KIWI

KICKS FOR GOAL

Hodder Moa

National Library of New Zealand Cataloguing-in-Publication Data

Lockyer, John, 1956-
Kiwi kicks for goal / John Lockyer ; illustrated by Bob
Darroch.
ISBN-13: 978-1-86971-079-8
ISBN-10: 1-86971-079-7
[1. Friendship—Fiction. 2. Kiwis—Fiction. 3. Birds—New
Zealand—Fiction. 4. Rugby Union football—New
Zealand—Fiction.] I. Darroch, Bob, 1940- II. Title.
NZ823.2—dc 22

A Hodder Moa Book
Published in 2006 by Hachette Livre NZ Ltd
4 Whetu Place, Mairangi Bay
Auckland, New Zealand

Designed and produced by Hachette Livre NZ Ltd
Printed by Everbest Printing Co Ltd

For more information about rugby, visit **www.ruggerland.co.nz** and **www.smallblacks.com**

KIWI
KICKS FOR GOAL

Written by John Lockyer   Illustrated by Bob Darroch

Kiwi could run fast. He could tackle, side-step and catch a ball. But sometimes when Kiwi played rugby he got nervous. So he worried when Coach Morepork chose him to be the Pipis' goal kicker for the next game. What if he missed?

Kiwi had seen the bigger players kicking goals at the park and he'd watched the All Blacks' kickers on television. His favourite kicker was Dan Carter. He made kicking goals look easy.

'Do you think I'll be a good kicker?' he asked Coach Morepork.

Coach Morepork blinked his big eyes. 'You never know how good you'll be until you try,' he said.

Kiwi had lots to learn. At home in the backyard, he kicked a ball over and over again.

'I hope I don't miss any goals,' he told his parents.

They smiled and said, 'If you practise, you'll be okay.'

Kiwi wasn't so sure.

The week before the game, there were many practices. Everyone wanted to improve their skills.

Kakapo hit the tackle bags. Kiore side-stepped the cones. Koura and Kea passed the ball.

'Great tackle! Excellent side-step! Speedy passing!' said Coach Morepork.

Pukeko and the other forwards made a scrum. They shouted, 'Heave!' and pushed against each other.

When Coach Morepork saw their heads up and their backs straight, he clapped and said, 'Magnificent!'

The Pipis practised lineouts. Kiore was the halfback so when Heron caught the ball he passed it to Kiore.

'Wonderful, wonderful,' said Coach Morepork. 'But where is Kiwi?'

Koura pointed at the goal posts.

Kiwi scratched his head. 'I want to kick the ball straight,' he said.
'But I can't. I don't know what I'm doing wrong.'
'Let's work together,' said Coach Morepork.

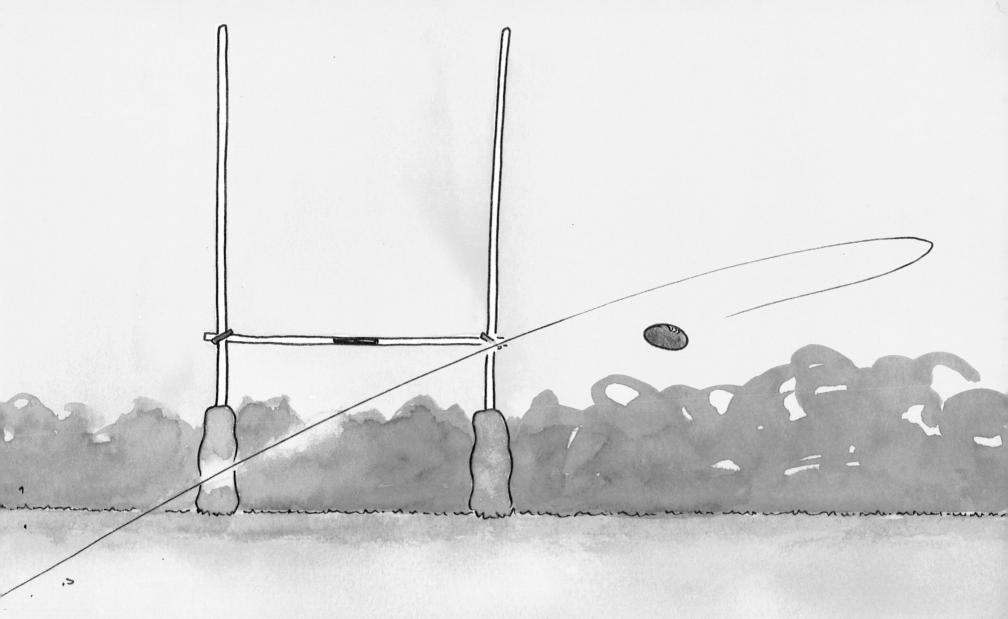

So Kiwi put the ball on the kicking tee. He stepped back then ran up and kicked the ball hard. It flew far away from the posts.

'Mmmm,' said Coach Morepork. 'We can fix that.'

Kiwi put the ball back on the tee.

'Keep your eyes on the ball,' said Coach Morepork.

Kiwi lined up the ball with the goal posts.

'Keep your eyes on the ball,' repeated Coach Morepork.
Kiwi stepped back.
'Keep your eyes on the ball,' he said to himself.
Kiwi ran up and kicked the ball hard. It flew high and fast and straight between the goal posts.
'Spectacular!' said Coach Morepork.

On the day before the game, Coach Morepork put the Pipis into two teams.

'For training today, we'll have a practice game,' he said.

Everyone tried their best. Heron leaped in the lineouts. Pukeko pushed in the scrums. Kakapo tackled down low. Koura ran fast and Kiore passed the ball quickly.

'Lovely skills,' said Coach Morepork. 'Now, Kiwi will show us what a fine goal kicker he is.'

Kiwi thought it was a good idea to practise
his kicking in front of others. He put the ball
on the kicking tee. But when he stepped
back he looked up and saw his team-mates.
Suddenly his tummy felt all fluttery.

'Go on,' said Kiore. 'Kick the ball.'

Kiwi knew what to do. He just couldn't get
his legs to move.

Kiwi was scared.

Coach Morepork talked quietly to Kiwi.
'You've got the collywobbles,'
he said. 'But that's okay. Remember,
keep your eyes on the ball. Forget
about everything else.'

Kiwi closed his eyes three times but each time he opened them he had to look away.

The fluttery feeling in his tummy was worse. So Kiwi asked Coach Morepork if he could take a break. That's when Pukeko said, 'Let me have a go. I can kick goals.'

Pukeko grabbed the ball. He tried to line it up with the goal posts but it wasn't straight.

Coach Morepork whispered to Kiwi, 'I think Pukeko needs help.'
So Kiwi straightened the ball. Then he said, 'Keep your eyes on the ball and step back with me.'
But Pukeko looked away then slipped over.

Kiwi said, 'Watch me.'

He ran up and kicked the ball hard. It flew high and fast and straight between the goal posts.

Everyone clapped and cheered.

'Your collywobbles have gone,' said Coach Morepork.

Kiwi laughed and said, 'I guess so.'

On game day, the Pipis ran fast. They passed quickly, tackled hard, pushed low in the scrums and jumped high in the lineouts. But the other team played just as well. It was a marvellous game but no one could score a try.

Then just before full time, in front of the goal posts, the referee blew his whistle and raised his hand. 'Penalty,' he said. 'Players are lying on the ball. What do you want to do, Pipis?'

Immediately, Kiore said, 'We'll have a kick for goal.'

And everyone looked at Kiwi.

Kiwi grabbed the ball. Then he saw his family in the crowd and his tummy felt a little fluttery. He took a deep breath. 'You can do it,' he told himself.

Kiwi put the ball on the tee. 'Keep your eyes on the ball,' he said.

He lined up the ball with the goal posts. He stepped back. He didn't see the Pipis or his family or the crowd. He didn't hear them whistling, cheering and clapping. All he saw was the ball.

Kiwi ran up and kicked the ball hard. It flew high and fast and straight between the goal posts. He'd done it.

The Pipis, cheering and laughing, ran to him. They grabbed him, slapped him on the back and heaved him into the air. Kiwi almost believed he was a great goal kicker like Dan Carter.

The Pipis shook hands with the other players then Coach Morepork gathered them around him. 'That was a great team effort,' he said. 'But our goal kicker won the game for us. Well done, Kiwi.'

Kiwi smiled. His tummy felt fluttery again but this time it was a warm, fluttery, good-all-over feeling.

And that evening, after a hot bath, Kiwi hung his Player of the Day medal on the wall above his bed. It had been a fantastic game — a game he wanted to remember.

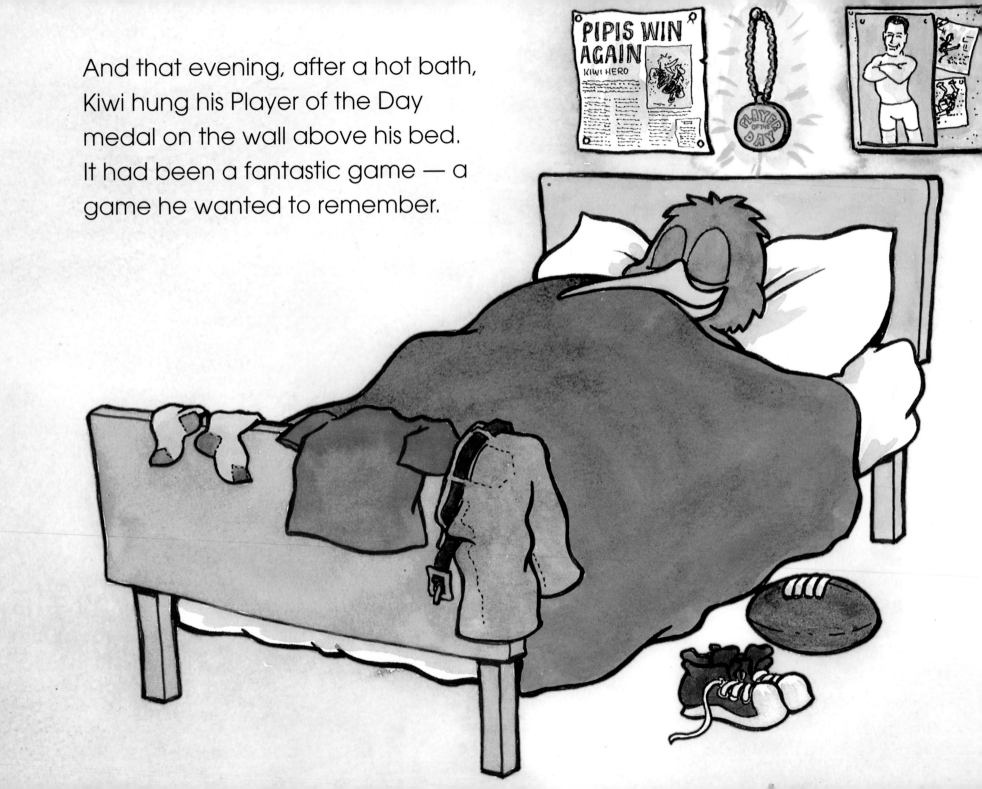